THE BOATING HOLIDAY

with Rufus, Granddad and Barney

written and illustrated
by Gerry Miles

HALSGROVE

For Karen and Justin

First published in Great Britain in 2012

British Library Cataloguing-in-Publication Data.
A CIP record for this title is available from the British Library.

ISBN 978 0 85704 190 6

Halsgrove
Halsgrove House
Ryelands Business Park
Bagley Road, Wellington
Somerset TA21 9PZ
Tel   : 01823 653 777
Fax   : 01823 216 796
e-mail   : sales@halsgrove.com

Part of the Halsgrove Group of Companies.
Information on all Halsgrove titles is available at : www.halsgrove.com

Printed in China by Everbest Printing Co Ltd.

Contents

4

Chapter 1

Today is the Day

The rooks flying around the tops of the tall beech trees call to one another to gather for their flight out to the fields. The big brown cockerel at the farm stands on a water pump, crowing loudly to his friends across the valley, their answering cries muffled by the mists rising from the damp meadows. The clock on the tower of the village church rings out four times.

Rufus listens to this dawn chorus lying in his bed, the sheets rumpled from tossing and turning. His excitement has been building over the last few days and he finds it impossible to sleep. He turns once more towards the faint glow at the bedroom window, but knows that it will be simply ages before he can get up.

The packing has already been done and the suitcases, bags and cardboard boxes are stacked in the hall ready to be loaded into the car. Perched on top of the pile is the handsome, radio-controlled, model fishing boat that Granddad had made him for Christmas. It was this beautiful present that had set Rufus to dreaming and today those dreams would come true.

He thinks back to that fine spring morning on the village green, kneeling on the grass, watching the red and yellow trawler bobbing across the ripples on the pond. He had turned to Granddad, sitting on the bench behind, and had told him how much he longed to go sailing on a real boat. Granddad had just nodded, but his eyes started to twinkle as an idea took shape. After a while, Granddad reached a decision, and to Rufus' surprise and delight, there on the village green, Granddad had promised that if Mum and Dad agreed, he would take Rufus on a boating holiday in the summer, and Granddad always kept his promises.

Needless to say, Mum was full of misgivings. She knew that Granddad had all the best intentions, but was still a boy at heart, and although Rufus had all his swimming diplomas, she was, none the less, worried about letting the two of them loose on a boat. Dad was also sceptical, but kept quiet and let Mum do all the talking. After a lot of passionate pleading from Rufus, and solemn promises from Granddad to be very responsible and take great care of his grandson, Mum had finally given in and said yes. Dad then also agreed, but insisted that the holiday would have to be a river cruise, since a trip out to sea would be far too dangerous.

Granddad and Rufus had started planning immediately and most evenings the lounge carpet was littered with maps of waterways and brochures for boating holidays. They read every single glossy pamphlet, studied the photographs and specifications of narrow boats and cruisers, and poured over charts of rivers and canals. Sometimes they were so engrossed in their searches and discussions, that much to Mum's annoyance, the steaming cups of cocoa she had made them went cold on the coffee table.

Eventually they came to a decision. Rufus fell in love with the picture of the "Lady Jane", a modern cabin cruiser with a smart red stripe down the side, advertised for hire by Smartboats Marina in Gosworthy. From this marina it was possible to sail down the River Mere through beautiful wooded countryside towards the sea. With a lot of help from Dad, the holiday was finally booked.

CRASH! There is an angry shout from the kitchen, followed by the slamming of the back door. Rufus is startled awake. He must have dozed off because daylight now streams through the curtains. He jumps

out of bed and runs down stairs in his bare feet, passing Granddad on the landing, stood in his pyjamas peering over the banister. Running into the kitchen, Rufus is greeted by Mum, standing with a mop in her hand, next to a broken pot and a puddle on the tiles.

"Since he's your dog, perhaps you would like to clean up the mess?

Mum's tone makes it clear that this is not a request.

Poor Barney, the excitement is infectious. All day yesterday in the hustle and bustle of packing, he had run round and round in circles, constantly looking up at Rufus in expectation, knowing that something unusual was happening, and hoping he would be part of it.

Rufus is the first to finish breakfast and leaves the table. He wanders over to the dining room window and looks out into the garden.

Barney is still banished from the house and is running furiously up and down the lawn. He hesitates when he sees Rufus at the window, but then careers off again. Barney is a young brown and white Springer Spaniel and is Rufus' constant companion. Like all Springers, Barney has absolute boundless energy and today he is like a coiled spring. First he races round and round the big flower bed at

the bottom of the garden and then rushes back the full length of the lawn to the patio where he spins on the spot, giving a comical skip as he twirls. Then he charges back down the lawn to run around the flower bed again. It makes Rufus tired just watching him.

"I wonder why Barney always spins and runs circles in the same direction?" he says.

"It's all due to magnetism," declares Granddad knowingly.

This makes Dad look up from reading the newspaper.

"Well," says Granddad, raising his hand to stroke his beard, " I read somewhere that if you empty a bath of water at the North Pole it swirls anti-clockwise down the plughole, and if you empty a bath at the South Pole the water spirals clockwise. I shouldn't wonder if Barney lived in Australia he'd run around in the opposite direction. It's all due to the earth's rotation!"

Mum looks at Granddad fondly and says, "You are a cuckoo!"

Granddad smiles mischievously and gives a chuckle.

"Maybe he's just left handed," says Rufus, still staring out of the window, and then adds, "In any case bathwater at the North and South Poles would be frozen and wouldn't run anywhere."

Dad grins and returns to his newspaper.

With breakfast out of the way it is time to pack the car. Fortunately, Dad has an estate car with plenty of space for their luggage. They not only have suitcases and bags packed with their clothes and toiletries, but there are also large boxes filled with groceries and other provisions.

While shopping at the supermarket earlier in the week, Dad grumbled that they had bought enough food to feed an army, but Mum was of the opinion that manning a boat is hard work and Rufus and Granddad would need all the nourishment they could get. Dad muttered that they were going on a river cruise and not fishing for cod on the high seas, but Mum would not be dissuaded.

Everyone is busy, with Dad, Granddad and Rufus shuttling backwards and forwards between the house and the car, while Mum busies herself in the kitchen making sandwiches and a flask of tea for the journey.

Just as they finish loading the car, their elderly neighbours Bert and Ruth peer over the garden fence to wish Granddad and Rufus a lovely holiday. Bert is a keen gardener and he proudly presents Dad with a basket of salad vegetables that he had picked earlier that morning with the dew still on them. Dad thanks him very much, then closes the back of the car, locks it with the remote and takes the basket into the kitchen.

"Bert is so kind-hearted," Mum says, looking at the basket full of delicious fresh lettuces, tomatoes and cucumbers. She takes it and places it on top of the refrigerator.

"Now you're sure you've got everything?" she asks Granddad and Rufus as they walk in.

"Absolutely," declares Granddad. "I've checked it all a hundred times, and I'm as sure as eggs are eggs that everything we need is in the car."

"What about your wellington boots and your rain jackets, I'm sure I saw them still hanging in the garage a short time ago?"

"Aaah!" says Granddad with an innocent look, "I was just about to get them."

Mum shakes her head in disbelief. "And what about your wallet?"

Granddad nods confidently, winks, pats his hip pocket, frowns, and goes off to find it.

"Dear me," sighs Mum, looking at Dad. "He'd forget his head if it wasn't screwed on tightly."

Dad shrugs. "Don't blame me, he's your father not mine."

By now Rufus is really anxious to leave and looks out into the garden.

"Where's Barney?"

The garden is empty.

They all troop out of the house and start calling him, but he is nowhere to be seen. They look behind the greenhouse and then the garden shed, but he is not there. The garden is fenced off and surrounded by high hedges so it is unlikely that he has escaped.

"Maybe someone left the back door open and he is in the house," says Mum hopefully, but a search upstairs and downstairs, looking in the most unlikely corners reveals nothing.

"He's picked the right moment to run off," says Dad irritably.

"He'd never do that," insists Rufus.

"Well, I don't know where he might be. There's nothing for it, I'll just have to take the car and drive around the village to see if I can find him."

As Dad opens the front door he laughs and says, "Well I never!"

They all look to where Dad is pointing, and there is Barney, stood up on the driving seat of the car, with his paws on the steering wheel, looking at them out of the windscreen. His tail is wagging furiously and they can hear his muffled barks through the closed windows.

"How the dickens did he get in there!" exclaims Granddad.

"Magnetism!" says Rufus.

Dad laughs. "Well now, if you two sailors are absolutely sure that you've got everything for your voyage, I think it's time to go."

Chapter 2

"Lady Jane"

The sun glints off of the river as they drive down the hill into Gosworthy and Rufus' heart begins to quicken. There stands the tall red sign for Smartboats Marina and Dad turns through the gates and parks in front of the Reception Office.

"This is it Ruuf!" says Granddad excitedly, giving Rufus a playful shove as he opens the car door. Barney springs right over Granddad knocking him back in his seat as he frantically scrambles to get out.

"Strewth!" says Granddad, straightening his shirt and brushing off the hairs.

They both step out into the sunshine and Rufus puts Barney on the lead as they follow Mum and Dad into the office.

"Hello, welcome to Smartboats," is the cheerful greeting from a pretty, young woman with a charming smile sitting behind a desk. She has long, blond hair and her face is peppered with freckles. She stands up and extends her hand. "I'm Mavis, have you made a reservation or are you just enquiring?"

"We've booked a boat," replies Dad, shaking her hand. He takes the booking documents out of a brown envelope and hands them to her.

She takes the papers, sits down and sorts through them and, after running her finger over the order form, types a number into the computer.

She looks up. "The booking is only for two people?"

"That's right," says Granddad, strolling up to the desk. "It's just for Rufus and me," and he cocks his thumb towards Rufus who is standing behind him, his face beaming with delight.

"And Barney!" says Rufus giving a pull on the lead, causing Barney to wag his tail and spin around.

There is a pause as Mavis looks at Barney and bites her lip. "I'm really sorry," she says apologetically, "But dogs are not allowed on our boats!"

There is a stunned silence and they all stare at her in disbelief. For a minute nobody can speak and Rufus feels a wave of disappointment wash over him. The day that was so bright and full of promise has suddenly turned grey and dismal.

The young woman breaks the silence. "I'm so sorry," she says again with deep concern, "but it does tell you in our brochure," and turning, she takes one of the booklets from a rack behind the desk. She opens it to the inside back page where Smartboats terms and conditions are listed. "It's item seven."

She hands the booklet to Dad.

He reads it slowly and shakes his head. "Oh dear, oh dear" he sighs, "we never saw that."

"Humph! That's torn it," mutters Granddad to no one in particular.

"I'm afraid there's nothing I can do," replies Mavis, coming from behind her desk and looking regretfully at Rufus.

Rufus sees the sympathy in her eyes and he turns, opens the door and walks outside. Barney seems to have caught the mood and trots meekly behind. Rufus slumps down on a wooden crate in the yard with a big lump in his throat, bravely fighting back the tears. Barney sits in front of Rufus and looks up at his sad face. Mum comes out of the office, puts her arms around his shoulders, hugs him to her and kisses the top of his head.

"Never mind," she murmurs, giving Rufus an extra squeeze. "I know it's a great shame, but I'm sure you and

Granddad will still have a lovely holiday."

Rufus looks at Barney who cocks his head to one side, and despite his best effort a tear rolls down his cheek.

"Hello! What's this then?"

A man is walking up from the jetty coiling a length of rope around his arm. He is dressed in blue, with a Breton cap, open-neck shirt and overalls. Despite the warm weather he wears wellington boots. He expertly ties off the coil, hangs it on the wall of the boat shed, then walks across the yard and stands in front of them with his hands on his hips.

"It's much too nice a day for such a long face. What's the matter?"

"We didn't realise that dogs aren't allowed on the boats," explains Mum, "and my son was really looking forward to taking Barney on holiday with him."

The man squats down and pats Barney on the head and ruffles his neck. "Hello Barney, you're a smart little chap aren't you?"

The man turns to Rufus, "And what's your name then?"

"Rufus."

"You've got a nice little dog, Rufus." And the man gives Barney another pat and tickles him under the ear. Barney lies down on his side and lifts one paw, enjoying the attention.

15

The man strokes his belly. "Springer Spaniels are a favourite of mine. Well behaved is he?"

"Oh yes," chips in Mum before Rufus has a chance to answer. "He's really no trouble and very obedient."

"Does he bark a lot?"

"No," says Rufus indignantly, finding his voice at last. "He was trained as a gun dog by my Uncle Steve. He listens very well and only ever barks if he gets really excited."

"He's a loveable dog and not at all aggressive," adds Mum.

"Well now." The man scratches the grey stubble on his chin and makes a soft clicking noise with his tongue as if considering what to do.

Just at that moment Dad, Granddad and Mavis step out of the office.

The man looks up. "What are we going to do about this Mavis? Can't have this boy going away on holiday on one of my boats with his face as long as a fiddle, can we?"

Mavis smiles.

"Tell you what Rufus, if you promise me that Barney will behave himself and not disturb other boats with a lot of barking and yelping, I'll let you take him with you. What do you say?"

"Oh, I promise, I promise, he'll be as good as gold," cries Rufus, his day suddenly brightening again.

Granddad lets out a whoop. "Yes, Yes!" and with a broad grin does a little jig.

"That's really good of you," says Dad. "I can't thank you enough."

"OK, that's settled then. I've spent the whole morning washing and scrubbing down the "Lady Jane" so let's go and have a look at her; she's the finest boat in my fleet. By the way I'm Harry," he says, shaking Dad's hand as they walk down to the jetty.

"Dennis!" says Dad, "and this is my wife Mary."

Granddad grips Harry's hand warmly. "Harry, you've made our day. Pleased to meet you, I'm Midge."

They cross to the floating jetty and Rufus breaks into a run, all cares forgotten as he sees the cruiser with the red stripe moored to a pontoon at the very end.

"One of the finest craft I've got," announces Harry for the second time as they all step on board the "Lady Jane". "She sleeps four so there'll be enough room for the two of you."

The cabin cruiser is a beauty with her decks gleaming and the chrome handrails glinting in the sunshine. Rufus lets Barney off the lead and he immediately spins round like a top, then jumps up and scampers along the deck to the bow, his toenails click-clacking loudly as he runs backwards and forwards.

"Barney! Here to me!" commands Rufus.

Barney skitters back.

"Sit!"

Barney does as he is told. He sits looking up intently at Rufus, who is holding his breath, worried that Harry might change his mind having seen Barney scurry about the boat.

"Barmy Barney," laughs Harry, and Rufus is relieved to see that he does not mind a bit.

Harry proudly shows them around. He starts with the cockpit at the stern of the boat that houses the steering wheel and controls. Three steps lead down to the first cabin, brightly lit by windows set high at deck level. To the left is a small galley with a cooking stove, refrigerator and sink. Polished wooden cupboards contain pots, pans, cups, saucers, and plates, and there is a drawer full of cutlery. To the right is a table with a white formica top and bench seats on each side to sit four people; the seat cushions are blue. On the wall above the seats is a detailed coloured chart to help with navigation and to pinpoint your position as you sail along the river. A red arrow marks the location of Smartboats Marina.

From the galley they step into a bedroom with a double bed fixed lengthwise to the wall and a wardrobe at the end for hanging clothes. In this bedroom there is also the same high window, but here the window has pretty curtains. On the bed are two pillows and a duvet with a paisley patterned cover.

Granddad sits down and bounces on the bed to test the mattress.

"That's just right," he murmurs in approval.

Next, a narrow corridor passes the washroom fitted with a toilet, shower cubicle and hand basin, and at the bow is the second bedroom. Here, two single beds on either side taper towards the prow with a low level cupboard built between them at the end. This bedroom is also light and airy.

Rufus turns around and looks at Granddad. "Looks like this is where I bunk down," he says, as pleased as punch.

Chapter 3

Manning the Lock

Harry proposes that as it is such a fine day it might be a good idea for him to first teach Granddad how to handle the boat before they stow all their luggage and provisions on board. He explains that there are many locks on the River Mere and that these locks, together with sluices and weirs, control the water levels in the river so that boats can navigate along its full length to the sea. The nearest lock is only half a mile downstream from the marina. Harry suggests that as soon as Granddad is able to safely steer and manoeuvre the "Lady Jane", that they set off down river to the lock where he will show Granddad and Rufus how it works. Mum and Dad are delighted when Harry invites them to come along for the short cruise.

Once they are clear of the pontoon Granddad listens carefully to Harry's instructions as he starts to steer the "Lady Jane" around the Marina. Granddad is a very practical person and has always had a good understanding of machines and he soon gets the feel of how the boat responds to the controls. With only a few light bumps and scrapes he quickly demonstrates to Harry that he is quite capable of sailing the boat and they set off along the river towards the lock.

Harry stands behind Granddad at the wheel. Mum and Dad bask in the sunshine on the wide cushioned seats at the stern and Rufus sits at the bow with Barney beside him.

Both Rufus and Barney are brimming with excitement at this new experience of sailing down the river on a beautiful boat. People strolling along the towpath wave cheerfully to Rufus, who waves back with a big smile lighting up his happy face, and if Barney's tail were to wag any faster it would surely fall off. Although it is now late afternoon the air is still warm and insects flit and hover above the water. Swallows and sand

martins skim and dart low across the surface feeding on this rich banquet.

It is not long before the lock comes into view. Under Harry's guidance, Granddad brings the cruiser smoothly alongside the landing stage in front of the lock gates and Rufus and Dad jump off and tie the mooring lines firmly to the bollards. Harry opens a cupboard, takes out a large metal crank handle and a key on a ring. They agree that it would be safer at the moment to keep Barney on the boat, so Mum slips the lead over his head and stays with him on deck.

"This is called a guillotine lock," explains Harry, pointing to the large, hanging gate in its steel frame at the far end. "Most of the locks on this river are of the same type. It gets its name from that big lock gate, which is winched up and down."

He gives Granddad and Rufus a meaningful look. "Now listen! It's very important for you to remember to leave the locks standing empty, with the swing gates closed." He pats the long arm of the swing gate that Rufus is leaning against. "It doesn't matter if you're sailing up or down the river, the guillotine must always be raised to the very top and secured and locked."

Granddad looks up at the tall gantry. "You mean we have to wind that big heavy door up and down by hand?"

"I'm afraid so," says Harry, smiling at the look on Granddad's face. "Let's start by lowering the guillotine and filling the lock. It takes about four hundred turns to lift or lower the guillotine, but it isn't that hard. If you and Rufus take it in turns to do a hundred each you'll have the gate down in no time."

"Big problem with that," says Dad.

"Oh, what's that?"

"Rufus can't count to a hundred."

"Dad!"

Rufus grapples him around the neck and laughing and yelling tries to wrestle him to the ground. Dad slips easily from his grasp, lifts him upside down and tumbles him onto the grass. Rufus jumps up, but Dad holds up his hands and grinning says, "That's enough!"

Harry shows them the key on the ring in one hand and the crank handle in the other. "Now these two items are very important so don't go losing them, otherwise you won't be able to operate the locks and you'll be stuck wherever you are."

He unlocks the winch and asks Granddad to start winding the large wheel. It turns easily and Granddad is able to lower the guillotine without any difficulty.

"Right," says Harry, "Now we have to fill the lock pen by opening the paddles in the swing gates. Rufus you come with me. Midge, you stay on this side."

Rufus and Harry cross the footbridge and when they get to the swing gate, Harry inserts the handle into a spigot on the top of the gate. The paddle is a small, sliding door in the base of the gate, and as Harry turns the crank the paddle opens and water gushes into the lock pen.

"Now don't do what I'm about to do," says Harry, and he throws the handle across the lock to Granddad. "It's a bad habit and if it accidentally falls into the river or the lock you won't be able to get it back!"

Granddad picks up the handle and opens the paddle in the other gate. The lock fills up surprisingly quickly and when the water level reaches the same height as the river the swing gates can be opened. Harry shows them how it is done.

"You have to put your back into it," he says, leaning against the arm of the gate and pushing backwards with his legs. Rufus takes up position beside Harry and together they push the gate slowly open.

"Right, now you Midge," he calls across to Granddad.

Granddad grunts, takes the strain, and before he has the gate halfway open, Rufus has run back across the footbridge to help him

"Piece of cake," boasts Granddad, puffing, with beads of sweat on his forehead.

Dad looks at his watch thinking about the long drive home and Harry realises that Dad is getting anxious about the time.

"I don't think we need to sail the boat into the lock, do we?" he suggests. "I'm sure you get the idea! We'll just go through the routine of closing and emptying it and once we've raised and secured the guillotine we'll go back to the marina."

Harry continues to explain the finer points of re-setting the lock and handling the boat during each stage, but Granddad and Rufus are so full of high spirits, they continuously laugh and joke and do not pay attention.

Chapter 4

A Sticky Problem

Back at the marina, Mum and Dad help Granddad and Rufus transfer the suitcases, bags and boxes from the car to the "Lady Jane" and Mum, being Mum, begins unpacking their clothes and stowing them away in drawers and cupboards. Unbeknown to Granddad and Rufus, as a surprise and special treat, Mum has brought along a two-pound jar of her homemade strawberry jam that she puts in the top cupboard of the galley. This is a big favourite with Granddad and Rufus, and Mum has twice won first prize with her jams at the village fete.

"Come on Mary," calls Dad. "They can do all that themselves, we must be getting off or it will be dark before we get home."

Standing on the jetty Mum gives Granddad and Rufus a big kiss.

"You will be careful won't you?" she says frowning and bends down and pats Barney on the head.

"They'll be just fine," says Dad getting a little impatient. He places a hand on Granddad's shoulder and hugs Rufus. "I'm sure you two are going to have the time of your life, we'll see you in a fortnight."

Reluctantly, Mum walks with Dad to the car and as they drive away she turns in her seat and waves until they are out of sight.

Harry unties the mooring lines and throws them to Rufus who coils them up neatly, just as Harry has shown him.

"Have a great holiday," he calls when Granddad starts the engine, "and take good care of my pride and joy," he adds, giving a wave. He turns and walks back to the office.

"Right!" says Granddad gleefully as they putter slowly out of the Marina. He starts whistling "A life on the ocean waves," and opens the throttle wider as they turn into the river.

Barney assumes his favourite position at the bow and shows keen interest in the many ducks, coots and moorhens paddling among the reeds and lily pads. Rufus stands beside Granddad, who is concentrating on steering the "Lady Jane" very carefully down the middle of the river. His lips are still pursed even though he has stopped whistling. He will not admit it to Rufus, but Granddad feels a little bit nervous now that they are on their own and Harry is not there to give advice or a helping hand.

It is late afternoon. Apart from a brightly painted narrow boat moored next to the towpath, there are no other boats to be seen and the walkers on the towpath seem to have gone home for tea. The sun is low in the sky as they approach the lock for the second time. Granddad throttles back the engine and guides the boat towards the landing stage. At the last moment he puts the engine in reverse, gives it a short burst and the cruiser's fenders gently nudge the dock. Harry would be proud.

"Well done Granddad!" calls Rufus as he jumps onto the staging and ties off the boat once again.

"Not bad, even if I say so myself," says Granddad beaming, his confidence beginning to return.

Granddad unlocks the winch and lowers the guillotine.

"I'll go and open the paddle on the other side," says Rufus, and taking the crank handle he runs across the footbridge. Once the paddle is open the lock starts to fill.

"Catch," he shouts, pretending to throw the handle over the lock to Granddad.

"Don't you dare!" shouts Granddad holding up his arm to shield his head.

"Only joking," laughs Rufus and runs back to open the other side.

Once the lock gates are swung open Granddad returns to the "Lady Jane" where Barney does a pirouette on the deck as he approaches and gives a sharp bark. He seems surprised and delighted to have found his voice and barks again.

"Less of that," says Granddad sternly, climbing back on board. "Just you behave yourself. Don't forget our promise to Harry!"

Rufus unties the mooring ropes and jumps on board and for the first time Granddad swings the boat out into mid-stream to line up with the entrance to the lock. He takes it very slowly and to his credit enters smoothly between the open gates. Rufus stands ready at the bow with the mooring rope in his hand and as they come alongside, he jumps off, slips the rope over the bollard and makes it fast.

"Nothing to it!" says Granddad, "I don't know what I was worried about," and he steps off to tie the stern rope.

Barney is getting restless having been confined to the boat all afternoon and wants to get off. He stands on his hind legs in the cockpit with his front paws on the step looking up at Rufus expectantly.

"No Barney. Stay!" commands Rufus, and Barney sits down obediently, although he looks a bit put out. He gives a big sigh, lies down and looks mournfully at Rufus.

"I should let him off," says Granddad. "We can't keep him cooped up on the boat all day. There's nobody about and he could do with a run."

"OK Barney! Come on then," beckons Rufus, and Barney springs over the side of the boat in a flash.

"What's next?" asks Rufus turning to Granddad. "Do we close the paddles and then shut the swing gates, or do we shut the swing gates and then close the paddles?"

Granddad raises his eyebrows and screws up his nose. "I don't think it matters as long as the paddles are closed before we raise the guillotine."

With both swing gates shut and the paddles closed, they stand at the winch ready to raise the guillotine. Barney stops running about and stands next to them watching the proceedings.

"I'll do the first hundred turns," says Rufus taking hold of the big silver wheel.

"OK," Granddad agrees, "but remember what Harry said about letting the water out slowly to begin with. Just give it a few turns and then wait."

Rufus turns the wheel and immediately there is a rush of turbulent water that wells up from under the guillotine. A few more turns and it becomes a powerful surge.

"That's enough for now," says Granddad as they stand watching the strong current of eddying water surging out of the lock. Granddad puts an arm around Rufus' shoulder. "We're really getting the hang of this aren't we?"

Barney suddenly barks loudly.

"What have I told…?"

Before Granddad can finish the sentence there is a sudden creaking groan, a crash of glass and china and a clatter of pots and pans.

They spin around and are shocked to see the "Lady Jane" hanging off the side of the lock at a steep angle, the mooring ropes stretched to breaking point as they strain under the full weight of the cabin cruiser.

For a moment they are frozen to the spot.

"Oh my lord!" shouts Granddad breaking the spell, and with great presence of mind he shouts, "Rufus,

close the guillotine!" as with remarkable speed he grabs the crank handle and runs to open the paddles.

Rufus spins the wheel with all his might and luckily, it being only partly open, the guillotine drops quickly to stem the flow of water escaping from the lock. Granddad furiously cranks open the first paddle and then runs down the length of the lock with Barney careering in front of him, then charges over the footbridge and down the other side as if his life depends on it. With the second paddle open and the water in the lock rising swiftly, he bends over coughing and spluttering with his hands on his knees. He puffs out his cheeks as the "Lady Jane" starts to float upright and the mooring lines slacken. With the danger past he leans against the arm of the swing gate, takes out his handkerchief and mops his brow while Barney tears round and round thinking that this is a fine old game.

The big rubber fenders have protected the side of the boat and the "Lady Jane" is once again floating serenely in the water as if nothing has happened.

Inside the cabin it is a different story. The galley cupboard doors have swung open and Granddad and Rufus are confronted with a jumble of pots, pans, plates, cups and saucers scattered over the floor and seats. Luckily they had not unpacked all of the boxes of groceries, otherwise there would have been a bigger mess. It is a miracle that, as far as they can see, only two cups, a tea plate and a jug have been broken. But there is strawberry jam everywhere! It is amazing how

far two pounds of deep red, strawberry jam can splatter when the jar falls out of a top cupboard and smashes on the edge of a table.

"Yes! Well!" is all that Granddad says as he closes the cabin door, shutting his eyes to the mess.

Standing together with Rufus in the cockpit he decides it will be better for them to sail out of the lock and moor further down river before cleaning things up.

As they set to work to empty the lock, Granddad loops the mooring lines once around two bollards and then stands in the middle holding both ropes firmly. As Rufus operates the guillotine he keeps the ropes taut, but gradually lets them slip through his hands as the water drains away. Gradually the "Lady Jane" lowers gently to the bottom of the lock pen. This time everything goes smoothly.

They find a suitable mooring not far down stream.

It takes quite a while to pick up all of the broken glass and crockery and mop the floor, but most of the time is spent with a bucket of hot soapy water and a dishcloth, wiping sticky jam off of the table, cupboards, walls and seats of the galley. When they have finished it all looks very clean and orderly, and the only evidence of the accident that remains is the faint, sweet smell of strawberries.

They have both been a little shaken by the episode, but have learned a lesson by it and are thankful that things have not been worse.

It is getting dark and Granddad boils a kettle to make a cup of tea. Their picnic lunch on the car journey with Mum and Dad is now a far off memory and after all the excitement they are absolutely starving. Barney is the only one who has been fed and he is curled up asleep in his basket under the table. It is very cosy in the cabin and Rufus also feeling tired, sits at the table and rests his head on his arms.

"So, what would you like to eat?" asks Granddad.

Rufus sits up and grins. "I'd like a jam sandwich!"

Granddad throws the wet dishcloth at him.

Chapter 5

The Weir

It is now two days since Rufus and Granddad operated their first lock and the scent of strawberries has at last disappeared from the galley. After passing through several locks on their way down the river they are getting very skilled at working them.

Granddad is as pleased as punch to pass on his newfound boat handling skills to Rufus and under his tuition Rufus can now steer the "Lady Jane" in and out of the locks, control the speed in forward and reverse and navigate with care when passing other boats. They have cruised along miles of the river with Rufus at the wheel, Granddad standing behind in case he gets into any difficulty. They are becoming seasoned sailors and their holiday afloat is turning out to be as wonderful as they had hoped.

The last two days have been sunny and warm and they have met lots of friendly boating people who have been very helpful in giving them tips and advice to make their life afloat even more enjoyable.

Last night they tied up against a busy quay alongside other narrow boats and cabin cruisers, where the river has been widened into a boating pool with a dock.

Rufus and Granddad sit out on the after deck munching their cornflakes as the early morning sun rises.

This is a very popular spot for pleasure boats and holidaymakers, with the neat, terraced lawns of the local pub "The Bargee" stepping right down to the towpath. Tables and chairs are laid out on the lawns under large sunshades, where several people are sitting enjoying a cup of coffee.

Further upstream water thunders over a large weir where part of the river spills into a stream, but it is far enough away to be just a background rumble.

A light wisp of a breeze makes the leaves on the trees shimmer as Granddad looks around him with a broad smile.

"Seeing all this green does your eyes good Ruuf."

"Does it?" asks Rufus.

"It certainly does, green's a very restful colour, it's a well known fact," and without further elaboration Granddad pours hot tea from his cup into the saucer, blows on it and slurps noisily.

"*My goodness,*" thinks Rufus, "*it's a good job Mum isn't here.*"

Granddad notices Rufus looking at him quizzically.

"Whaaat?" He draws the word out slowly.

"Nothing," says Rufus shrugging his shoulders.

"Oh this!" laughs Granddad raising the saucer and grinning. "What the eye doesn't see, the heart doesn't grieve over," and leaning back in his seat, he stretches out his legs.

"Does tea taste better out of a saucer Granddad?"

"It's another one of those well known facts Ruuf," he says winking, and then muses, "That's what holidays are all about; relaxing and doing the things you just like doing."

Barney comes and sits down next to Rufus and nudges his elbow with a cold wet nose, his eyes raised questioningly. Rufus, who has a mouth full of milk and cereal, realises that Barney has not yet been fed. He quickly swallows the mouthful and jumps down the steps into the cabin, returning with Barney's bowl and a packet of dog biscuits. He shakes out a generous portion.

"Here we are Barney," says Rufus, walking to the front of the boat and putting the bowl on the deck.

Barney is not the tidiest of eaters and scoffs greedily, scattering biscuits all about him. Some biscuits fall over the side into the water attracting a group of hungry ducks that are on constant alert for tasty morsels. Barney finishes up the stray biscuits around the bowl, and then pricks up his ears at the sound of the ducks in the water squabbling over the crumbs. Oh, what fun! He cannot resist the temptation, and before Granddad or Rufus have time to react, Barney leaps off the side of the boat and lands with a big belly flop,

right into the middle of them. Ducks scatter, splashing and squawking, in all directions, the water frothing as they streak away in panic.

All that is, except for one little brown duck, who swallows down the last crumb and casually paddles away with her tail feathers bobbing tantalizingly in front of his nose. This is like a red rag to a bull and Barney swims after her in full pursuit, the duck paddling steadily ahead, just far enough to keep out of harm's way.

"Barney, come back here this minute!" shouts Rufus, leaning over the rail, but to no avail. The duck lures Barney further and further up the river.

Granddad and Rufus jump from the boat and run along the towpath shouting and whistling, but Barney keeps on swimming, his ears deaf to their calls.

"Oh my goodness!" exclaims Granddad, as the duck glides across the wide river heading straight

towards the edge of the thundering weir. A broad band of water in front of this roaring cascade is as smooth as a mirror where the strong current picks up and sweeps over the edge.

Hearing their anxious calls and seeing the imminent danger, other people join in the shouting and whistling, but duck and dog swim purposefully on towards the weir.

"What can we do Granddad?" pleads Rufus.

Granddad shakes his head in despair, "I've no idea Ruuf." And they look on helplessly as Barney swims on, oblivious to the peril.

The shouting stops. Everyone holds their breath, riveted to the spot.

Rufus stares in disbelief, anxiety welling up inside.

Just before the duck reaches the mirror edge of the strong current she flaps her wings and flies away over the waterfall leaving Barney floundering in the water.

Barney looks about him, then turns around and starts to paddle back. At first he does not seem to make any headway, but he is a strong swimmer and gradually, to everyone's great relief, he draws away from the weir and the danger zone.

Some people on the riverbank start cheering, while others still call and wave their arms frantically. As Barney gets closer Granddad stops biting his fingernails. Rufus cannot stop laughing as he hops up and down on his toes, clapping his hands with joy.

There is quite a reception as Barney clambers out of the river and climbs up the steep bank. He shakes himself briskly showering Granddad and Rufus.

Rufus flings his arms around Barney's neck and gives him the biggest hug, and Barney licks his face not knowing what all the fuss is about, but enjoying all the attention. Smiling people pat Rufus and Granddad on the back and shake their hands, congratulating them on Barney's safe return.

When all the excitement has died down, Granddad and Rufus walk slowly back along the towpath to the boat with Barney trotting to heel.

Climbing on board they slump down on the seats quite exhausted from Barney's narrow escape.

Some quacking ducks glide by and Barney pricks up his ears.

"Don't even think about it!" warns Rufus sternly.

Granddad goes down into the galley. "I'm going to put the kettle on, I need a strong cup of coffee to calm my nerves. That's quite enough excitement for one day, thank you!"

But how wrong he is!

Chapter 6

The Bridge

The weather forecast has reported heavy rainstorms across the country and there has been extensive flooding in many places. Luckily for Rufus and Granddad, although it has sometimes been cloudy, until now every day of their holiday on the river has remained fine and dry, and today is no exception. They can see that the river level is rising, which must be due to floodwater coming down from the far away hills. It has almost reached the top of the lock gates in places and on some stretches the river has spilled over into the water meadows.

Granddad and Rufus are still a little uptight and jumpy from Barney's early morning swim with the duck. A group of ducks are swimming around the quay scrounging tit-bits from the people on the boats and more of them are waddling between the tables on the pub lawns, hoping for scraps from holidaymakers now enjoying breakfast. In order to avoid more trouble, should Barney get it into his head to take another plunge, Rufus has shut him in the galley.

With a light breeze ruffling the water they make ready to cast off and as they pull away from the dock several people wave goodbye.

Very soon they are sailing through open countryside with the wide river meandering between fields of waving corn. For as far as the eye can see there are no other boats or locks in sight.

A plaintive bark reminds Rufus that Barney is still in the cabin and since they are underway, he lets him out. Barney is delighted to have his freedom back and runs down to his favourite position at the bow.

Granddad swivels in the seat and asks, "Do you think you can handle the boat on your own for a while Ruuf, while I go below for a wash and brush up?"

Rufus cannot believe his ears. His eyes light up and his wide grin gives Granddad his answer.

"Right Ho then!" says Granddad, standing up.

He holds the wheel while Rufus raises and adjusts the seat and then Rufus sits down and takes control.

"That's the ticket. Keep her at a steady speed and just give me a shout if you need me." Granddad ducks his head and disappears into the cabin.

Oh boy! This is what Rufus has been dreaming of since Christmas. Captain Rufus! How cool is that? Here he sits in charge of this beautiful cabin cruiser with the ship's wheel held firmly in his hands. He is thrilled to bits that Granddad thinks he is good enough to take control of the "Lady Jane" single-handed. He looks expectantly left and right along the banks of the river, but there is no one around to witness his first solo voyage. Even Barney is not interested, sprawled out on deck lazing in the sunshine.

He can hear Granddad through the skylight of the washroom giving himself a good scrub in the shower, the cares of this morning forgotten. He is singing a sea shanty about a drunken sailor at the top of his voice, occasionally tapping out the rhythm on the walls of the cubicle.

A narrow boat comes into view around a bend in the river, painted in red, green and yellow, with colourful, floral patterns on the cabin doors. A black terrier standing on the roof sees Barney and barks excitedly. Barney sits up, gives a single bark in reply and looks back at Rufus as if to say, *"Well, you've got to be friendly, haven't you?"*

Rufus steers to one side to give the barge a wide berth, and as the boats pass the man at the tiller waves to Rufus and shouts something about a bridge. Rufus cannot hear what he says above the noise of the engines, but nods his head as if he understands and waves back.

Dark clouds gather temporarily blocking the sun as the "Lady Jane" enters the wide sweeping bend that curves around a line of tall weeping willows, whose long slender branches reach down as a pale, green curtain to the water. The current seems to be flowing a little faster, but Rufus senses no immediate problems and steers back to the middle of the river. Barney is suddenly alert at the bow and cocks his head to one side, looking keenly ahead.

Suddenly, emerging from behind the screen of trees, an impressive stone bridge comes into view, spanning the river in three arches. Having been hidden by the trees as the boat rounded the bend, the bridge is quite close and it is clear to see how much the river is swollen. There is not much headroom under the archways and the strong current churning around the stone buttresses creates high bow waves that curl away to form deep troughs. On either side of the river the banks are lined with boats with not a single space between them, and a crowd of people gathered on the bridge point excitedly as the "Lady Jane" approaches.

"Oh no!" gasps Rufus, gripping the wheel tightly as the boat picks up speed.

Barney creeps in from the deck and cowers on the floor sensing that something is wrong.

Granddad, oblivious to the pending danger, is singing at the top of his voice and drumming on the washroom door. "Put him in the scuppers 'til he's sober, put him in the scuppers 'til he's sober…"

Things have happened so quickly that Rufus is in panic and sits glued to the seat with his mouth wide open not thinking to call Granddad for help.

Luckily the "Lady Jane" stays in the middle of the river, and at the last moment, as the widest arch looms large, the sun breaks through lighting up the bridge and the boat plunges into the darkness. .

Rufus closes his eyes, grips the wheel with white knuckles, and lets out a frightened "Oooooh!"

There is a long, loud, metallic clatter and scraping, and Granddad's singing stops. Then all is quiet except

for the rumble of the motor.

Rufus dares to open his eyes and looks behind; blinking, he sees that by some miracle the boat has sailed safely under the bridge.

Granddad rushes into the cockpit, his face half covered in shaving foam, and rescues the wheel from Rufus' shaking hands. Upon hearing his plaintive cry, followed by the loud clattering and scraping, Granddad had leapt from the washroom fearing the worst. Seeing the bridge the colour drains from his face as he realises that they must have just sailed through that low, dark, narrow, archway.

"You all right, Ruuf?" he asks anxiously, looking into Rufus' frightened eyes.

Rufus stares at Granddad, but manages a nod.

Granddad raises his eyebrows and blows out his cheeks. "Phew!"

Rufus moves out of the swivel seat, and Granddad guides the boat to the riverbank and cuts the engine.

Some of the people that were standing on the bridge are now running down the towpath towards them.

"Good Lord," puffs a fat man with a red, florid face. "That was a fine display of boatmanship if ever I saw it. We've been discussing all morning whether it would be safe to sail under the bridge with the river in full flood and you shot through without hesitating!"

Granddad splutters through a mouthful of shaving foam, "Well, we, um…" But the people are looking at Rufus who had been the only person on deck as the "Lady Jane" had swept under the bridge.

Rufus sheepishly bows his head and says nothing.

A young man, seeing the bent and buckled aerial on top of the cabin, gives Granddad a knowing look, much to his embarrassment.

A man in a red anorak, wearing sunglasses, strokes his chin while weighing up the situation and declares. "I think you've been pretty lucky, I'm going to wait another day before I attempt to sail under the bridge."

Granddad coughs and clears his throat. "Well! It's been very nice meeting you all, but we must get on."

As the crowd disperses and the people start walking back towards the bridge, a well-meaning lady hangs back and says to Granddad, "Don't worry about it dear, we all make mistakes."

Barney pokes his head over the side to watch them go, his nose twitching nervously.

Chapter 7

The Luxury Cruiser

Granddad is woken up early by sunlight shining into his cabin. He was so tired last night after yesterday's dramatic events, that when he had finally crawled under the bed covers he had forgotten to close the curtains. He pulls off the duvet and gets up. There is no sound from Rufus' bunk, and Granddad dresses as quietly as he can so as not to disturb him.

Barney is out of his basket and as soon as he sees Granddad he spins like a top, his tail thumping loudly on a cupboard door at every turn.

"Shusssssh! You little perisher," whispers Granddad.

He opens the cabin door and steps up into the cockpit. Next he unfastens and folds back the dark blue, canvas hood that protects the afterdeck, and having tucked and stowed the hood neatly away, he steps off of the boat onto the riverbank. Barney jumps after him and immediately rushes about, tail wagging, his nose close to the ground. He darts through a hole in the hedge into a field, surprising a family of rabbits, but Barney has more urgent things to do than chase rabbits. Coming back to the riverbank he finds a suitable tree and cocks his leg.

There is still no sound from Rufus.

Because there is a chill breeze on the river this early in the morning, Granddad pulls on a thick jumper, makes himself a cup of coffee, goes back outside and sits down on the stern seat. Barney settles at his feet.

Granddad notices a family of swans feeding quite close to the boat. There are five cygnets with brown, downy feathers grouped together under the protection of their parents. One swims in front of the youngsters and one at the back, constantly alert for any threat to their brood. The graceful adult swans, pure white with

orange bills, swim serenely and effortlessly in the current. Occasionally they duck their heads underwater, using their long necks to nibble at the weed and sift through the mud and gravel of the riverbed. As they dip their heads in the water and bob down to feed, they look quite comical with their tails stuck straight up in the air, their large webbed feet paddling to keep them in position.

Granddad clicks his tongue and in response the swans cautiously move towards the boat thinking that he has some food. They are a little uncertain and it takes some time for them to cross the river. The cygnets still keep in close formation and make soft peeping noises as they swim nearer. Granddad keeps clicking his tongue as encouragement.

Just as they reach the side of the boat, up springs Barney to have a look at what Granddad's doing and all hell breaks loose. The cygnets scatter and the male swan rears up and hisses loudly, spreading and flapping its huge wings. Barney yelps in fright and jumps back bumping into Granddad, who spills the remains of his coffee over the deck.

"If that isn't the last straw," declares Granddad grumpily, the peace of the morning having been so abruptly ended.

The swans drift downstream on the current out of harm's way and the baby swans are quickly ushered back into a tight group as the parents restore order.

A bleary eyed Rufus sticks his head out of the cabin door. "What's all the noise about Granddad?"

"There are times when I could cheerfully strangle your dog," mutters Granddad, checking to make sure he hasn't spilt any coffee on his trousers.

As they motor along an attractive stretch of the river, cloud shadows chase across meadows speckled with buttercups and daises, and the yellow flowers of wild iris brighten the riverbank. A herd of cows have come down to a muddy watering hole to drink, some standing knee deep in the water, tails swishing to ward off the flies. They gaze quite unconcerned as the "Lady Jane" passes.

Granddad is letting Rufus pilot the boat this morning so that he can get his confidence back after the fright of sailing under the bridge. Granddad is quiet and lost in thought. Boating is great fun and they are having a wonderful holiday, but messing about on the river has its dangers. The troubles of yesterday have reminded him that the river demands respect and it is up to him to take more care.

Eventually, the beauty of the river scenery and the cheerfulness of the people that wave to them from passing boats lifts his spirits and he starts humming a tune. Rufus looks up at him and smiles.

As they round a bend in the river between densely wooded banks, they come to yet another lock next to an old watermill. Although they have already negotiated two locks that morning and are getting really efficient at it, Granddad is still very wary and double-checks everything.

They are just about to close the swing gates behind them when a horn toots from up river. An enormous luxury cruiser has just rounded the bend and a man standing at the bow is hailing them.

"Ahoy there!" he shouts in a posh voice, "Don't close the gates, we're coming in too."

Granddad has misgivings as to whether there is enough room for both boats in the lock pen, but he and Rufus wait patiently as they approach.

It is a magnificent boat and the four people on board are very smartly dressed. The two men have matching peaked caps and yellow windcheaters; one woman wears a colourful dress, the other, a bright top with shorts. It all looks very shipshape and professional and Granddad is really impressed.

"We'd better not make any mistakes with these experienced sailors around," says Granddad. "Let's pull "Lady Jane" up closer to the guillotine to make more room, it's going to be a very tight fit."

The young man standing at the bow has a coiled rope in his hand and as they near the lock he climbs over the chrome railing in readiness to jump off. Unfortunately, without realising it, as he climbs over, the short flagpole on the prow slips up under the back of his windcheater.

"There's not a lot of room," shouts Granddad.

"It'll be quite all right old chap, don't worry!"

The older man at the helm puts the engine into reverse to slow their speed as the big boat glides alongside. The man with the coiled rope jumps, but to his and everyone's amazement, instead of landing on the quayside he is left dangling from the flagpole by his jacket, his legs kicking and flailing wildly.

Rufus bursts out laughing at the comical sight, but quickly realises that the man is in serious trouble.

Under his full weight, the collar of the young man's jacket tightens around his neck and starts to choke him. The older man rushes to his aid, but is unable to lift him from the flagpole.

Granddad runs across the footbridge to help, while Rufus jumps from the "Lady Jane", and clambers over the railings onto the deck of the big cruiser.

The man's face is turning blue as they hoist him by his armpits off the flagpole. He is still gasping and choking as they drag him back to safety. He lies on the deck rubbing his sore neck.

After sipping some water he is able to speak, but his voice is quite croaky when he thanks Granddad and Rufus for their help.

Once all the commotion has settled down the lock gates are closed, but it is a very tight squeeze.

At both ends of the lock pen there is a yellow stripe with a notice saying "Do not moor in yellow zone", but

the prow of the "Lady Jane" is very close to the Guillotine door and the sternpost of the "Wanderer", for that is the name of the big cruiser, is almost touching the swing gates at the other end. There is absolutely no room to move.

Rufus stands holding the mooring lines as Granddad raises the guillotine.

All goes well until the lock is half empty. Green water begins to trickle through a gap between the swing gates where through age they have warped and sprung. As the water level in the lock drops further the gap widens and the trickle becomes a torrent, and then as the pressure increases a powerful spout gushes through the misshaped doors straight into the after deck of the 'Wanderer". The two boats are jammed in so tightly that it is impossible to move the cruiser out of the way of the foul stream. The ladies, who in the meantime have gone down to the galley to search for the medical box, let out piercing shrieks as dirty water pours down the steps and swamps the cabin.

Granddad winds the winch like a madman to raise the guillotine as fast as he can, but by the time they are able to sail out of the lock, the cabin of the "Wanderer" is knee deep in river water.

You have never seen such a forlorn sight. The smartly dressed ladies are soaked to the skin. The older one is wringing her hands and near to tears; the younger one is bent down consoling the injured man who is still sitting on the deck rubbing his neck. The elderly gentleman looks completely bewildered.

The boats are now tied up to the landing stage.

"Is there anything we can do to help?" asks Granddad.

"No! No!" exclaims the elderly gentleman somewhat embarrassed. "This is entirely our own fault, we insisted on coming into the lock with you. It's very kind of you to offer, but we'll sort it out. You've been a tremendous help already. No! No! You carry on and enjoy your holiday".

As Granddad and Rufus cast off from the landing stage, tempers flare behind them and a heated argument breaks out.

"Oh lor'!" says Granddad, feeling really sorry for the elderly gentleman. "Sounds as if he's got a mutiny on his hands".

Rufus bends down to make a fuss of Barney. "Well done Barnacles you didn't bark once during all the fuss!"

The rest of the day passes without incident, and that evening they sail into a short half-mile section of the river between two locks. Having had quite enough of operating locks for one day they decide to moor up for the night.

Chapter 8

The Storm

That evening a chill settles on the river and heavy clouds bank up as it begins to get dark. They raise the hood, secure it with the clips and ties, and as they zip up the door to shut out the cold the first spots of rain patter on the canvas.

Granddad prepares a stew and when this is simmering in the pot and the potatoes are boiling the galley gets nice and warm and the windows steam up. By the time they sit down to eat, the rain is much more persistent and the wind is blowing in strong gusts.

There is a low rumble.

"It looks like we're in for a storm," says Granddad. And as he speaks there is a flash of lightning followed by another grumble of thunder.

"Will we be safe in a thunderstorm on a boat?" asks Rufus.

"Safe as houses," says Granddad. "In any case the storm's quite a long way off. With luck it'll pass us by."

"How do you know it's far away?" asks Rufus, not convinced.

"When you see the flash of lightning you count the seconds until you hear the thunder. Every five seconds is a mile."

They sit and wait in silence.

Flash!

Granddad counts, "One and two and three and four and…" The thunder rolls out. "There we are, four and a half miles! 'Course it's not accurate, but it gives a good indication."

Rufus finishes up the last delicious morsels of stew on his plate.

"Is there any more?" he asks, licking his lips.

"Sorry Ruuf, that second helping was the last of it," replies Granddad, pleased that Rufus is enjoying his cooking.

Another flash.

Rufus counts, "One and two and three…" The storm is coming closer.

Together they clear the table and start the washing up. Granddad washes and Rufus wipes.

Rain drums harder on the roof and the flashes of lightning with crashes of thunder are becoming more frequent.

Barney is getting agitated and cannot settle. He darts nervous glances at Rufus as he patters round and round in circles.

"What game would you like to play this evening?" asks Granddad as they sit back down at the table.

"How about draughts?" says Rufus. It is one of his favourite games.

Granddad reaches into a drawer and takes out the chequerboard. As he does so the drumming of the rain becomes an insistent hammering with metallic pings. The noise is so loud that they can hardly hear themselves speak.

"Hailstones!" shouts Granddad above the din.

Barney is now under the table cowering between their legs.

Rufus is startled by a brilliant flash that lights up the galley, and jumps out of his seat and under Granddad's protective arm as the whole boat shudders from a deafening boom, followed by an ear splitting crackle that sounds as if the sky above their heads is being ripped open. Granddad hugs him close and Barney lets out a long pitiful howl.

They can smell the electricity in the air.

"I don't like it Granddad."

Granddad holds Rufus tight to comfort him and waits for the eye of the storm to pass.

When everything has quietened down they have a cup of cocoa and then go to bed. Rufus lies in his bunk listening to the rain, but there is no longer any sound of thunder. Satisfied that the storm really has passed, he pulls the cover up to his chin, turns on his side and closes his eyes.

The chequerboard lies on the galley table with the box of wooden playing pieces left unopened.

They both stand looking up in astonishment at the large oak tree. It has a wide white scar with black scorch marks running down from the crown to the base. One of its boughs has been struck by lightning and has crashed to the ground blocking the towpath. It is still attached to the trunk by a splintered stump.

"That was close," says Granddad, looking back at the "Lady Jane" not fifty yards away. "It must have happened last night when that giant clap of thunder shook the boat."

"I thought you said we'd be safe in the boat?" says Rufus questioningly.

"Well we were, weren't we?" is Granddad's positive reaction, and looking back up at the tree, he adds, "It never does to underestimate the power of nature."

The storm seems to have cleared the air. The morning is fresh and bright, the sky blue and streaked by high, wispy clouds and the birds are in full song.

"Listen to the birds singing," says Granddad. "They were out in that storm all through the night and they're not complaining!"

After the heavy rains it is clear that the river is swollen and has risen still further, the water level getting close to the tops of its banks. The mooring ropes are taut and the "Lady Jane" is tilting slightly, so they slacken them off.

Granddad suggests that after weathering the storm they deserve a good breakfast and they sit down to eggs, bacon, sausage and baked beans.

"There, that'll put hairs on your chest," says Granddad proudly, placing the full plates on the table, while Rufus opens the tomato ketchup.

They have a leisurely breakfast and of course the conversation is all about the thunderstorm. By the time they have washed up, cleared away the breakfast things and taken Barney for his morning walk, it is half-past-ten before they are ready to cast off. Unusually, they have not seen another boat pass by.

It is not far to the next lock and when they arrive at the landing stage and step off, it is obvious that there is something wrong. There are three boats tied up to the downstream staging waiting to enter the lock to sail up river and Granddad and Rufus join a group of people stood looking at the swing gates. The river is so high that the tops of the gates are submerged and the river sweeps over them creating a formidable waterfall.

"Good morning," says a blond-haired man with a serious expression. "I'm afraid you won't be able to go any further down river today. We've tried to operate the lock, but as you can see, when it's filled, the river is so high that the water overflows and it's impossible to open these swing gates against the current. What's it like upstream, are the locks still passable?"

"I have no idea," answers Granddad. "We were only moored a little way upriver and this is the first lock we've come to."

The blond man turns to his wife. "There's nothing for it love, we'll just have to find a mooring somewhere for the day and come back tomorrow to see if things have improved."

The people wish them good

luck and return to their boats.

Granddad considers their options.

"Since we've only got a few more days holiday left Ruuf, I think it might be better if we turn around and start making our way back to the marina."

Rufus looks a bit crestfallen.

"Cheer up me old mate," says Granddad, "Let's stay positive, it's just as much fun sailing up the river as it is sailing down."

The river is not very wide at this point and it takes Granddad several attempts to turn the boat before they are able to sail back upstream. When they reach the lock that they had passed through the previous afternoon, they are faced with yet another powerful waterfall cascading over the lock gates. They are trapped and can sail no further.

"Well this is a fine kettle of fish," says Granddad. "It looks as if we're up the creek without a paddle."

They have no choice but to return to their overnight mooring by the stricken oak, where the metal stakes are once again driven into the soggy riverbank and the "Lady Jane" is made fast.

Chapter 9

The Village

Despite the setback and disappointment of being stranded between the two locks, the sun is shining and the day is warming up. Across the valley the spire of a church and the tiled and thatched roofs of houses can be seen among the trees. Between the river and the village there is a large lake crowded with ducks, geese and swans, and the sunlight shimmers and sparkles on the ruffled waters. Because of its regular shape, Granddad thinks it may be a flooded gravel pit.

Since they need fresh milk and their stock of food is running low, Granddad decides that they should walk to the village and suggests that Rufus takes along his model boat to sail on the lake. When they are ready to leave, Granddad picks up the haversack and pats his pocket to make sure he has his wallet. Rufus emerges from the cabin carrying Barney's lead with the fishing boat tucked under his arm.

At the lakeside a notice states, "Wildlife reserve. No swimming or fishing. Dogs must be kept on a lead." But at the first sniff of water Barney has already run ahead and is gaily splashing about in the shallows with the ducks and geese giving him a wide berth. He has picked up a stick and dropped it at the water's edge for Rufus to throw.

"Come here Barney!" calls Rufus, and when Barney runs out of the water, Rufus slips the lead over his head.

Barney looks at the stick and then back at Rufus.

"Not today," says Rufus.

Granddad thinks that there is no harm in Rufus sailing his model boat on the lake and sits in the sunshine on the bank stroking Barney to keep him quiet. Rufus takes off his trainers and is soon lost in the pleasure of sailing the little trawler along the channels in the reed bed, guiding it in and out of the harbours formed by gnarled tree roots that spread out into the crystal clear water. Minnows skitter across the sandy bottom between his bare feet.

Continuing their walk beyond the lake they cross a narrow, wooden footbridge over a stream, after which the well-worn path to the village skirts along hedgerows, where butterflies flit among the wild flowers. A field of wheat has been flattened by the heavy rain and gusty winds of last night's storm, but bright red poppies still stand bravely at the edge.

They climb over two stiles before stepping out into a country lane, where a signpost directs them to the village of Upper Filton, half-a-mile.

On the outskirts of the village, they approach "Bramble Lodge", a lovely thatched, stone cottage with a mass of pink rambler roses growing around the porch. The garden is a riot of colour and a lady in a broad brimmed hat is busy at work in a crowded flower border, tying up tall delphiniums and hollyhocks that have been knocked over by the heavy rain.

A chocolate Labrador runs to the garden gate, pokes its nose through the bars and gives a deep, throaty bark.

"That's enough Amy," calls the lady, who turns round and gives them a smile as they pass.

"Good morning," says Granddad.

"Afternoon," she corrects him, looking at her watch. "It's ten past one."

"Is it as late as that?" questions Granddad, stopping and looking at his own watch. "Goodness, I don't know where the time's going today!"

"I know what you mean," sympathises the lady, removing her gardening gloves. "I've taken up the whole morning tidying the garden after that awful storm last night." She takes off her hat and tousles her hair. "Wasn't it dreadful? Living on my own as I do, I don't mind admitting that I was quite scared. Amy howled at the top of her voice at every clap of thunder and I sat in the kitchen gripping the arms of my chair, convinced the house was going to be struck by lightning."

Barney has pulled Granddad to the garden gate and is making acquaintance with Amy with much sniffing and licking.

"The storm's caused us problems as well, hasn't it Ruuf?"

Rufus nods his head and kneels down at the gate to make a fuss of the dogs, who are getting along just fine.

"We're on a boating holiday," explains Granddad, "but with the river flooded by the storm, the water's so high we've got stuck between locks and can't sail either up or down the river. Is there a shop in the village where we can buy some groceries?"

"Yes! Of course," she says enthusiastically. "You can get everything you need at the Post Office. Margery will be able to sort you out. Just carry on down the road past the church and you'll find the Post Office a little further up on the right, opposite the farm."

"Thanks very much."

While Granddad has been talking to the lady, Barney has been fidgeting, turning round and round in front of the gate, hoping that someone would open it. He has twisted the lead, and Granddad has to untangle it before they can walk on.

"I've just thought!" exclaims the lady. "Margery closes for lunch between one and two, so you'll have a bit of a wait I'm afraid."

Rufus' tummy rumbles. "I'm getting really hungry," he says, speaking up for the first time.

The lady smiles at him. "Well now that's easily put right, there's a nice tea shop at the farm where they have really lovely sandwiches and cakes, I'm sure you'll find something there to satisfy you."

Granddad thanks her again and they set off for the village.

Amy gives a parting bark and Barney looks back wistfully, sorry to leave his newfound friend.

Rufus' eyes are as big as saucers as he looks at all the homemade cakes on display in the tearoom and reads their names. Chocolate Gateau, Lemon Drizzle, Date and Walnut, Dundee Fruit Cake, Victoria Sponge and Carrot Cake: what a choice.

Rufus decides on a slice of Chocolate Gateau and a glass of orange juice and Granddad orders a pot of tea, a ham sandwich and a piece of Carrot Cake.

"I'll bring the ham sandwich to your table as soon as it's ready," declares the girl behind the counter.

They find a table by the window and sit down; Rufus places his model boat on the floor by the wall, where it will not get damaged.

When the ham sandwich arrives it is made from thickly cut, farmhouse bread and comes with a mixed salad and potato crisps.

"There you are," says the waitress. "Can I get you anything else?"

"No, I think that will be quite enough," answers Granddad beaming at the feast set before him.

Rufus looks at the piled plate and then at Granddad.

"I'm a growing boy," protests Granddad.

"You're growing all right," jokes Rufus patting Granddad's belly.

"Well, you cheeky blighter!" and with that Granddad picks up Rufus' chocolate cake and pretends to take a bite.

"Hey, give it back," cries Rufus, but Granddad holds it just out of his reach.

Rufus grabs Granddad's carrot cake and really does take a bite out of it.

"OK! OK! I give up," laughs Granddad, and puts Rufus' cake back on his plate.

A little girl sitting with her Mummy at the next table is giggling at their antics.

"Mmm! That's really nice," says Rufus in surprise. "It doesn't taste of carrots at all."

"Well, before we tuck into the cakes, are you going to help me out with this ham sandwich?" asks Granddad.

"Yes please."

Barney has been tied up outside the teashop in the shade and has been given a bowl of water. He is quite happy and gets lots of attention from the teashop customers.

By the time they have finished lunch the Post Office is open and a bell jangles as they open the door.

"Hello!" calls a plump woman in a pink overall as she busies herself with a display of greetings cards.

"Hello Margery!" calls Granddad as if he has known her all his life.

She looks across at Granddad with a puzzled frown.

"Do I know you?" she asks.

"No," replies Granddad, "The lady at "Bramble Lodge" gave us directions and mentioned your name."

"Oh, that'll be my friend Felicity Brown. How can I help you?"

"We just need some milk and a few groceries," says Granddad picking up a plastic basket from the stack by the door.

"Just give me a shout when you're ready then," she says, and carries on sorting the cards.

The shelves in the village shop are well stacked and there is a good assortment of things that they need. Soon the basket is full and they go to the checkout.

"Oh! What a cute Springer Spaniel!" exclaims Margery, bending down to give Barney a pat. "What's his name?"

"Barney," says Rufus.

"I love Springers, they're such friendly little dogs; they have so much energy and are always on the go. My Dad was a gamekeeper and always had Springers. He used to say they're hardworking and obedient, but completely crazy."

"Barney certainly lives up to the crazy bit," says Granddad.

Margery starts to empty the items out of the basket scanning the labels. Granddad holds the haversack open and Rufus fills it with the assortment of packets, bottles and tins that they have bought.

"What brings you to Upper Filton?" asks Margery.

"We're on a boating holiday and…"

"MY BOAT!" exclaims Rufus, hastily giving Granddad Barney's lead and rushing out of the shop.

"What's that all about?" enquires Margery.

"I think he's left his model boat in the tearoom," says Granddad, packing the last few items.

Margery hands him the payment slip. "That'll be thirty-seven pounds and five pence."

The bell clangs and Rufus marches back in with his precious boat.

"Now that's what I call a boat," says Margery admiringly. "It's a good job you remembered where you left it, it would be a real shame to lose that."

Rufus holds the boat up proudly for her to see. "Granddad made it for me as a Christmas present."

"My word! You are a lucky boy to have such a clever Granddad."

Granddad's face turns pink.

"So you're on a boating holiday?"

Granddad explains that they are stranded between two locks because of the flooded river, and tells Margery of his concern that they have to get back to Smartboats Marina by mid-day Saturday.

Margery's response is very matter-of-fact. She puts her hands on her hips. "Well it can't be helped can it? It's not your fault! If you're still stuck here on Saturday, Harry Smart will have to come here, pick you up in his car, and take you back. He can sail his boat home when the river's gone down and the locks are clear."

"That's true enough," agrees Granddad. "So you know Harry then?"

"Lord yes! Everybody around here knows Harry. He's the salt of the earth. We used to go to school together."

Margery looks out of the window at the blue sky. "The weatherman on the T.V. last night said that the heavy storms are heading north and that we're in for more settled and sunny weather. I shouldn't think you'd have long to wait before the river goes down and the lock gates clear. Why don't you do a spot of fishing in the meantime," she suggests. "It seems a shame to sit on a boat all day long with nothing to do and nowhere to go."

"That would be great," pipes up Rufus eagerly.

"It's a nice idea," nods Granddad in agreement, "but the trouble is we've got nothing to fish with."

Margery smiles. "I think I might be able to help you there, I'll just have a hunt about in the storeroom."

After a few minutes she comes back with a reel of nylon fishing line, a card with different sizes of fishhooks, and a plastic float. "We don't get much call for this anymore since they opened the big fishing tackle shop in Brampston, I thought we still had some lying around."

"That's marvellous," says Granddad rubbing his hands together. "How much do I owe you?"

"Just thirty-seven pounds and five pence," she insists. "The fishing line and hooks are my treat."

She beckons them with her finger to come closer, and although there is no-one else in the shop, she whispers, "Now I'll give you a bit of advice. My husband always says that the best fishing is in the little stream that you crossed as you walked to the village. Follow it upstream from the lake until you come to a little stone bridge; that's the best spot. With any luck you might catch yourselves a nice trout."

"You're really kind, thank you very much," and Rufus leans forward and kisses her on the cheek.

Margery is a little flustered by his show of affection and ruffles Rufus' hair. "Oh! Don't mention it, it's my pleasure." She opens the shop door.

"Bye, Bye my dears!" she says cheerily. "Don't worry your heads about the floods. Enjoy the rest of your holiday and good luck with the fishing."

Chapter 10

Tickled Pink

It is a balmy evening, in sharp contrast to the raging storm of the previous night. Instead of driving rain and blustery winds, the air is now warm and still. Stars are out and a crescent moon shines down on Rufus and Granddad, as they sit on deck drinking their cocoa. It is very quiet; the only sounds to be heard are the murmur of the river and the croaking of a frog somewhere out on the lily pads.

Moths flutter around the lamp in the cockpit as Granddad takes one of the middle-size hooks from the card and ties it to the end of the fishing line. He then attaches the red plastic float a little further up.

"Do you know much about fishing, Granddad?" asks Rufus.

"Do I know much about fishing?" declares Granddad indignantly, and then laughs, "No, not a lot."

"What are we going to put on the hook as bait? Do you know what fish eat?"

"Margery said we might catch a trout, and they eat flies and other insects. We could catch one of those moths, but I think the best we can do is dig into the riverbank in the morning, and see if we can find some small worms."

"Worms aren't insects," says Rufus.

"No, but they wriggle about a lot and might attract a fish. For fly-fishing you need a special fishing rod so that you can skim the fly across the surface of the water." He flicks his wrist to demonstrate. "Mind you, if you're skilled enough, you don't need any fishing tackle at all."

Granddad finishes tying on the float and looks up. "When I was a boy the local poachers used to catch trout with their bare hands"

"How on earth did they do that?" asks Rufus.

Granddad wiggles his fingers. "They tickled them."

"Tickled them," snorts Rufus, thinking that Granddad is telling him another one of his tall stories. "I suppose the trouts died laughing?"

"No, listen, I'm serious. You'd be amazed how clever those poachers were."

Granddad tells him that where he grew up as a young lad there were chalk streams full of trout. Rich men paid a lot of money to go fly-fishing on those rivers and water-keepers with dogs and shotguns guarded their fishing rights. The last thing a poacher wanted, was to be found by a keeper with a rod, line and net, because if caught they would be fined and jailed, so they developed a way of catching trout by hand. It took lots and lots of skill and patience.

The poachers knew that the fish rested and sheltered under stone ledges and overhangs, so they would lie down on the riverbank where they were hiding, dip their arms into the water, and slowly feel along with their fingers. If they touched a fish, they would stroke its belly, caressing it gently with their fingers until the fish went into a kind of trance. When their hands were right underneath the fish they would suddenly grab it tight and flip it onto the bank.

"Wow!" exclaims Rufus. "That's incredible."

"It certainly is," says Granddad. "I've never actually seen it done, but I know it's true."

Granddad carefully pushes the fishhook into a wine cork and puts the fishing line into a plastic bag. He drains his cocoa. "It's getting late Ruuf. We'll just wash up these two mugs and then get to bed, shall we?"

Rufus looks at the riverbank. "The river doesn't seem to have dropped at all, does it?"

"No sense worrying about it," says Granddad, pulling up the hood ready for the night. "Trout for supper tomorrow."

It is very quiet and peaceful. Rufus leans against the low parapet of the old stone bridge, one elbow planted firmly on the top of the wall, his head resting on his hand as he gazes down into the clear waters of the stream. Barney lies panting in the shade at his feet, finally tired of chasing butterflies and bees and anything and everything that moves. Long strands of waterweed wave gracefully in the current and a family of coots search for food among the reeds at the water's edge. The dappled sunlight breaking through the leaves of the tall trees sparkles on the water and dragonflies skim over the surface; brilliant blues and greens glint from their lacy wings as they flit in and out of the bright patches.

The model fishing boat that Rufus has been sailing under the bridge lies on the wall beside him.

Granddad's eyes are closed, his face turned upwards to the sun. He takes a deep breath and gives a long, contented sigh. He sits on top of the wall in the middle of the bridge next to Rufus, his hands resting at his sides, and his legs, with trousers rolled up to the knees, dangle over the edge. He twitches his foot, tickled by a fly, and this jiggles the fishing line tied to his big toe. The line disappears into the dark water under the bridge. To Rufus it seems hours since the wriggling worm was set on the hook and he is getting bored and is ready to go back to the "Lady Jane". He is daydreaming about a strawberry jam sandwich and a glass of orange juice. He wrinkles his brow.

"I still can't see any fish Granddad," he complains.

"Mmm?" Granddad opens one eye and gazes down at his grandson. "Fish are smart Rufus; they're hiding under the bridge."

"It's really dark under there. Perhaps we'd have been better off using a glow worm?"

"Humph!" is the only reply and Granddad closes his eye.

Rufus makes his mind up. "I'm going for a stroll down the river Granddad. I'll leave my boat here."

Granddad nods with his eyes still closed. "Don't go too far," he says.

Rufus steps out along the path and Barney runs back and forth sniffing and snuffling in the undergrowth. After a while they come to a shady spot where the path passes between hazel thickets. Branches laden with nuts hang out over the stream where the riverbank is sculpted into shallow pools between the roots of the trees. Thick, long grass grows on the bank. It is not a strawberry jam sandwich, thinks Rufus, but a few fresh hazelnuts would make a tasty treat. A cluster of nuts is within easy reach and Rufus clings on to a sturdy branch to steady himself as he leans out over the water to pick them. With his arm outstretched something catches his eye and he glances down. He stops and holds his breath. There, in the clear eddying water under the overhang of the bank, a large speckled fish is resting in the shade. He pushes himself slowly back, all thoughts of nuts forgotten.

Barney comes bounding along the path from where he has been digging frantically at a rabbit hole.

"Shush Barney! Stay!" says Rufus in a loud whisper, holding his finger up as a warning.

Barney sits down on the path and cocks his head to one side inquisitively. Rufus kneels down on the riverbank above where the fish is hiding, peers over the edge, but can see nothing. Barney lies down on the path, his tail still wagging, but a Springer Spaniel can never stay still for one moment and he starts to creep forward.

Rufus is tingling with excitement. Now what had Granddad said exactly about tickling a trout? Everything must be done in slow motion. He lies down and stretches out in the long grass at the edge of the overgrown bank, hoping that the fish is still there. He nervously bites his bottom lip, and with trembling fingers gently dips his arm into the cold water.

What next? He resists a shiver, cups his hand in the water with his fingers pointing upwards and begins to wiggle them. Surely the fish has seen his arm by now and has swum away? He moves his hand slowly towards where the fish should be resting and another thrill runs through him as his fingers brush against something. Whatever it is, it is alive, because it is gently moving against the rhythm of the current. It must be the fish. Unbelievable! His fingers caress its belly, and it seems to take forever as he gradually inches his hand towards the head of the trout, constantly moving his fingers. The fish has stopped moving and he expects it to dart away at any second. He is concentrating so hard on tickling the trout that as his fingers finally stroke the fish's gills - the hot, slobbery lick on his ear makes him jump out of his skin.

"WHAH!" he shouts in alarm, but instinctively grabs hold of the fish and without thinking jerks it out of the water onto the bank, where it flips and flops among the grass and fallen leaves.

Rufus sits up with his heart pounding, while Barney barks wildly, springing around the jumping fish, patting it with his paws. By the time Rufus has recovered from the shock, the fish has stopped flipping and flopping and is lying still on the grass with its mouth gaping. Barney gives it another prod, but out of the water it is too tired to struggle. Rufus takes a closer look and sees how beautiful it is. So sleek and shiny with its silver flank speckled with all the colours of the rainbow. As Rufus carefully removes pieces of grass and leaves that have stuck to it, its large round black eye seems to stare balefully up at him and he realises immediately what he must do. He picks it up, steps into the stream and gently places it back in the water. The trout lies quietly cradled in his hands for a few seconds, and then quickly swims away.

When Rufus gets back to the bridge, Granddad is still sitting in the same place jigging his leg up and down in the hope that the fish will take the bait.

"Caught anything yet?" calls Rufus.

"Not even a nibble. Did you have a nice walk?"

"Yes thanks," replies Rufus, deciding not to tell Granddad about the trout that he had caught and then let go. After all, Granddad has been sitting patiently on the bridge all day long trying to catch one and wouldn't understand.

"I'll give it another ten minutes and then we'll go," says Granddad.

"OK, I'm going to sail my boat under the bridge for the last time," and with that Rufus runs down the bank.

Kneeling on the grass, Rufus places the brightly painted boat in the water, and as many times before that day it bobs and sails away under the bridge. He quickly scrambles up the bank with Barney barking and rushing ahead, skips across the narrow lane and slides down the bank on the other side to steer the boat as it comes out of the dark tunnel. Barney has already jumped into the river and is splashing about barking with excitement, each bark echoing loudly under the bridge.

"Keep him quiet," shouts Granddad, "He'll scare all the fish away."

The boat appears, but for some reason it doesn't respond and drifts to the middle of the stream out of reach. The batteries need recharging.

"Oh no!" shouts Rufus, seeing that his lovely boat will be lost and swept away, but Barney comes to the rescue, plunges into the deeper water and swims out to the middle of the stream to retrieve it. Just as he reaches the boat he gives an almighty yelp, turns around and swims for the shore. By the time he climbs out of the river he is howling in pain because the fishing line is firmly hooked in his tail.

As Barney runs up the bank, Granddad twists around on the wall to see what all the fuss is about. At that very instant, Barney's tail is yanked tight, the line goes twang and Granddad gives a startled "Whoops!" as he loses his balance and falls off the bridge into the river. Rufus rushes onto the bridge and looks over to see Granddad sitting in mid-stream nursing his toe. He looks a comical sight with his head covered in green waterweed.

"Are you alright Granddad?" shouts Rufus.

"What do you think?" complains Granddad with a pained expression. But looking up and seeing Rufus'

worried face, he smiles and says, "I'm OK Ruuf, nothing's broken".

He removes the weed from his head, unties the fishing line from his toe, stands up in the middle of the river, and with a disgruntled frown, folds his arms.

"Well that's a fine end to a day's fishing, I must say."

Rufus helps Granddad out of the water and they sit down together on the grass bank. As Granddad pulls on his socks and rolls down his soggy trousers, they are suddenly aware of Barney's whimpering and whining.

"Oh, poor Barney," says Rufus," I forgot about him."

They find Barney on the grass bank, licking his tail, with the fishhook still firmly embedded in it.

"Let me have a look, old chap," says Granddad kindly, as he gathers Barney in his big arms. Very carefully he prises the hook out of his tail; Barney licks his ear to say thank you. Granddad winds up the fishing line and sticks the hook in the cork to make sure no one else can get caught in it.

Walking along the footpath back to the "Lady Jane", Granddad still looks a sorry sight in his sopping wet clothes. His shoes make squelching noises and leave damp footprints.

Rufus' shoulders are slumped and he lets out a big sigh. "I can't believe it Granddad. I've lost my lovely boat."

They had searched up and down the banks of the stream but could not find it.

"Never mind Ruuf," says Granddad, taking his hand and giving it a squeeze. "I'll make you a bigger and better one."

Granddad sighs as well. "The other disappointment today is we haven't got a tasty trout for supper."

Rufus thinks back to that beautiful streamlined fish with the rainbow speckles and is pleased that he let it go.

Barney runs ahead of them, tearing in and out of the hedgerows, his tail wagging furiously even though it still hurts a little bit.

Chapter 11

High and Dry

Rufus is still feeling a bit down in the dumps after losing his model boat, but he soon perks up when, after breakfast, Granddad says he can take the helm and sail to the upper lock to see if they can make their escape. Their hopes have been raised this morning by the fact that the mooring lines are slack and it is obvious that the river level has dropped a little.

First the "Lady Jane" has to be turned around, and for Rufus this is the best part. Earlier in the week it had taken him seven moves, going backwards and forwards until the boat was facing in the opposite direction and he had occasionally bumped the riverbank while attempting this difficult manoeuvre. Even though Rufus thought that Granddad bumped the banks just as hard as he did, Granddad tut-tutted and said, "Careful Rufus, we don't want to put a hole in her."

After two days of practice, Rufus can now turn the cruiser around in three moves, one better than Granddad, who says that this is because he wears glasses.

Stood at the wheel steering the "Lady Jane" is still a magical time for Rufus and the cabin cruiser glides through the water parting the wisps of white mist that still cling to the river. A heron is startled by their approach and rises with powerful wing beats from the riverbank as they draw near to the upper lock, with its guillotine standing sentinel at the entrance.

Something has changed, but what?

Why! Of course! There is no waterfall tumbling over the lock gates, which means they can open them and get through.

"Whoopee!" they cheer, and Barney does a pirouette on the bow.

Granddad is full of smiles as they busy themselves with the lock. He is so relieved that they can start

sailing back to the marina, because they only have two full days of their holiday left and he knows that it is a long distance to cover in a short time.

Granddad studies the river chart on the wall of the cabin. "We're really going to need a full head of steam," he remarks.

Rufus looks puzzled. "Shall I put the kettle on?"

"No!" chuckles Granddad. "What I mean is, if we're going to get back to Smartboats Marina by Saturday, we're going to have to make tracks!"

Rufus is still confused. Steam? Tracks?

"There will be no time to stop along the way," explains Granddad. "We will press on today until nightfall to get as far up river as we possibly can."

They make first-rate progress and travel up the river much faster than they had sailed down. Rufus handles the boat very well and they work efficiently as a team to get smoothly through the locks. Barney soon learns to keep out of their way after getting tangled in Granddad's legs, sending him sprawling across a footbridge. Some choice words were spoken that cannot be repeated.

The river is busier than usual. Many boat owners want to take advantage of the first day that the river has been navigable since the big storm. There have been queues at some locks and people have been very excited and keen to exchange stories of their experiences during the flood. Even so, by six o'clock that evening, they have managed to cover more than half the distance to the marina.

Rufus and Granddad are proud of their achievement and as the sun begins to dip over the horizon they look for a suitable place to tie-up for the night.

They find an idyllic spot on a very wide stretch of the river and hammer the metal stakes into the riverbank. As they tie off the mooring lines the last rays of the sunset send up a red and orange glow that fades into the deep inky blue of the night overhead. A string of purple clouds hang motionless above the

84

horizon, their edges tinged with gold.

They are tired but happy and sit on deck eating their supper in complete silence, content to just watch the sun go down. Mugs of steaming cocoa finally finish them off, and when they climb wearily into their beds they fall fast asleep as soon as their heads touch the pillow.

Rufus is awoken early in the morning by an enquiring "woof" from Barney in the galley. As his head clears, he blinks, rubs the sleep from his eyes and listens.

"That's strange," he thinks.

The boat seems to be gently rocking in time with a scraping noise coming through the side of the hull close to his head.

Granddad is still fast asleep, snoring like a foghorn as only Granddad can.

Now wide-awake, Rufus sits up and draws back the curtains, and then kneeling on the bed, he wipes away the condensation from the window. He cranes his neck to peer outside, but it is very misty in the early morning light, and although the scraping noise continues and the boat keeps rocking, he cannot make out what is causing it. He slips on his body warmer and walks through to the galley where Barney greets him excitedly. He then steps out into the cockpit, pulls on his wellington boots and unzips the canopy.

Once outside he steadies himself with one hand on the

damp railing and leans over it to look forward; to his surprise, a large black and white cow is scratching its backside against the side of the boat.

He jumps down onto the riverbank and runs towards the cow waving his arms shouting, "Shoo, shoo!"

Barney races ahead, but then suddenly realizes that this is a very big cow and thinking better of it darts back behind Rufus. The cow seems quite unconcerned by Rufus' behaviour and ambles slowly off across the meadow with her heavy udder swinging between her legs. She then stops and turns her head to look at Rufus and Barney with large, sorrowful eyes. Rufus ushers her further away to discourage her from coming back to scratch some more.

He turns back to the boat and his mouth drops wide open and his eyes stare in disbelief at the scene that faces him. The boat is no longer in the water, but sits high and dry on the riverbank.

Once the enormity of this sinks in, he yells, "GRANDDAD!" at the top of his voice, and runs back to the boat and clambers on board.

He clatters down the steps to the galley and bursts into Granddad's bedroom, grabs his shoulder and shakes him, shouting "Granddad, Granddad, Granddad. Wake up! You'll never believe what's happened!"

Granddad gives a snort, rolls over and opens his bleary eyes, slow to react to the sight of Rufus frantically jumping up and down and jiggling about in front of him. This rude awakening is made worse by Barney's loud and excited barking that adds to the din.

"Good grief!" yawns Granddad, quite confused as he looks about him.

"Come on Granddad you must get up," shouts Rufus desperately.

Granddad clambers awkwardly out of bed and then coming to his senses he stiffens and sniffs the air in alarm. "Is the boat on fire?"

Rufus shakes his head. "No, no, come and see!"

"We don't seem to be sinking?"

Rufus grabs his hand and begins to tug him along to emphasise the urgency.

"Granddad, it's unbelievable, we're stuck on dry land! The boat isn't even in the river; it's sitting in the field!"

With Rufus pulling his arm and Barney joining in by tugging at his pyjama leg, Granddad stumbles outside.

"Oh my lord," he groans, taking in the situation. "How is this possible?"

He had carefully measured the depth of the water under the boat before they had tied up at the mooring and there had been plenty of clearance. For some unknown reason the river level has dropped dramatically during the night, gently lowering the "Lady Jane" onto the soggy grass. Unwittingly, little knowing that they were not actually in the swollen river, they had moored above the flooded bank.

Looking underneath the boat Granddad can see that the keel has settled deep in the soft mud. Tantalizingly, the river is only an arm's length away, but the cruiser is well and truly stuck fast. The boat weighs more than a ton and there is absolutely no way they can move it.

Granddad climbs back on board, sits down and flicks his bottom lip with his finger. He then puts his head in his hands and sighs.

"Only one thing for it. We will have to ring Harry to tell him what's happened."

"He's not going to be very happy," says Rufus, stating the obvious.

"No," mutters Granddad. "How would you feel if you picked up the telephone and someone blurts out, *"Sorry Harry, your pride and joy's no longer in the river, we've managed to park it in a field?"*

He looks at Rufus and gives an embarrassed laugh.

Granddad takes a deep breath and stands up. "Ah well, it's too early to do anything about it now, we'll have some breakfast and then go and find a telephone."

"Mum's always saying you should have a mobile phone."

Granddad prickles. "Yes, but this is not the time to remind me Ruuf."

Chapter 12

Slipping and Sliding

Granddad enters the telephone booth, while Rufus and Barney stand outside, but Rufus holds the door open so that he can listen to the telephone conversation. Granddad puts in some coins and dials Harry's number. Luckily, it is Harry who answers the phone and not Mavis.

Harry listens without interrupting as Granddad explains what has happened. When he has finished his woeful tale, Granddad braces himself for Harry's angry response.

Instead, Harry seems quite unruffled. After a short pause he says in a reasonable tone, "The Mere's a tricky old river when she's flooded Midge. You weren't to know it, but last night, as an emergency measure, the Water Authority opened all of the sluices along the full length of the river in order to drain the floodwater away. It's almost unheard of; the river must have dropped a good six feet

overnight. You're not alone. I've had calls this morning from two other boats in trouble. Although I must admit, you're the only ones who managed to get their boat stranded high and dry on the riverbank. Where are you exactly?"

After Granddad has given details of where the boat is marooned, Harry tells him not to worry, it is not the first time that this has happened and because the "Lady Jane" is so close to the water's edge, he believes she can be winched back into the river using a tractor. He says it will take him a couple of hours to get things organised and he will come down personally to supervise the rescue.

Rufus and Granddad walk the half-mile back to the boat and wait.

It is mid-morning before Harry arrives, driving across the field in his Land Rover and drawing up alongside. As he steps out Granddad greets him with a nervous handshake.

Granddad is sincerely apologetic. "Sorry about this Harry."

Harry shrugs his shoulders, "Can't be helped, we'll soon have it sorted out."

"I must say you're being very reasonable about the whole business."

"Well Midge, the way I see it, you must have had quite a turn this morning when you discovered you were stuck. It wouldn't have improved the situation if I'd flown off the handle, would it? Besides, it's your first time on the river and the flooding over the last week is some of the worst I've seen in years. I've wondered once or twice if you were all right. If you'd had a telephone I would have rung you."

Granddad looks disgruntled as Rufus gives him an I-told-you-so look.

"How are you young feller me lad?"

Rufus screws up his nose and looks at the "Lady Jane" feeling really awkward. "I'm fine thank you."

Harry crouches down. "And what about you Mister Barmy Barney, how much mischief have you got yourself into since I saw you last?"

Barney is plastered in mud from running about in the soggy ground. He rushes up to Harry who,

90

laughing, rolls him over and gives him a vigorous rough and tumble.

Harry steps down the bank and looks along the boat to take in the situation. "Let's have a look at the lie of the land," he says, examining the underside.

After a careful assessment he comes to the conclusion that it should be fairly straightforward to get the "Lady Jane" re-floated. He takes out two spades from the back of the Land Rover and explains that he wants to dig away the soft earth from under the front end of the boat, so that he can place some large, round logs crosswise underneath the keel. As the tractor pulls the "Lady Jane" off of the bank, she will skid over the logs without sinking further into the mud.

They set to work, Rufus and Granddad glad to be doing something useful to help get the cruiser back into the river. It takes half-an-hour for them to hollow out enough space to set five sturdy pine logs in place under the hull and while they are working, a huge, green tractor with enormous tyres, drives into the field on the other side of the river.

Harry and the tractor driver Dave stand on opposite banks and shout to each other across the

river, discussing where to position the tractor so that the winch will give the most effective pull. They agree that the tractor should be parked about fifty yards further up the riverbank so that the towing cable will be stretched diagonally across the water. This will take care that the "Lady Jane" will slide lengthwise from the bank into the river.

Dave throws a coiled rope across to Harry, who on the third attempt manages to catch it with a boat hook. The rope is tied to the end of the heavy winch cable and Harry and Granddad haul it over. Harry then clambers on board the "Lady Jane" and attaches the cable to anchor points on the deck. Granddad and Rufus untie the mooring ropes and pull the stakes out of the ground.

With the tractor in position, Dave starts the engine, engages the winch and slowly takes up the slack. When the cable is taught, Harry checks to make absolutely sure that it is securely fastened, and once satisfied, he gives Dave the signal for operations to begin.

Harry has asked Rufus to keep well away, and he stands watching at a safe distance with Barney on the lead. He has every faith that Harry and Dave know what they are doing, but keeps his fingers crossed behind his back for good measure.

The tractor engine revs up to a higher pitch as the cable takes the strain. At first there seems to be no movement and then the "Lady Jane" begins to inch forward. As Harry had expected, the logs prevent the hull from nosing deeper into the ooze. She gradually begins to slide forward and then gently skews sideways .The bow dips into the water and the cruiser swings out into midstream like a pendulum, still held fast by the cable.

Dave stops the winch.

There is a familiar rumble as the engine of the "Lady Jane" comes to life and Harry steers the boat back to the riverbank.

Rufus and Granddad hammer in the stakes and then make the "Lady Jane" fast, while Harry releases the winch cable and Dave winds it in.

Harry cups his hands around his mouth and shouts, "Thanks mate!" to Dave, who puts his thumbs up. Then Dave starts the tractor and with a final wave drives off.

Granddad and Rufus help Harry to tidy up the riverbank, dig out the logs that are embedded in the mud and put them back in the Land Rover. Then Granddad puts on the kettle and after washing their hands, they sit down in the galley with a cup of tea.

"I hope this experience hasn't put too much of a damper on your holiday?" asks Harry.

"It has been a bit of a set back," admits Granddad, "but my goodness we have had a wonderful time. Haven't we Ruuf?"

"Great!" says Rufus. "I just love the "Lady Jane"; she's the best boat ever!"

They finish their tea and since it is now mid-day, Granddad asks Harry if he would like to stay for a spot of lunch. Harry thanks him, but says that he had better be going because he has had another urgent call from a family on one of his other boats. It seems that they have managed to get a rope wrapped around their propeller.

"No peace for the wicked," he chortles. "Listen! I'd appreciate it if you'd try to get back to the marina before twelve o'clock tomorrow. That'll give me time to get the old girl cleaned and spruced up for my next customers."

Rufus is not happy thinking about other people sailing on the "Lady Jane".

The holiday is coming to an end.

Chapter 13

Landlubbers Again

They have moored overnight about two miles from Gosworthy with only the last lock separating them from the marina. Last night Granddad took very great care with the soundings, but with the river almost back to its normal level there was little risk of making the same mistake twice. In way of thanks to Harry for being so understanding about getting stuck on the riverbank, Granddad and Rufus have decided to give the "Lady Jane" a complete spring clean from top to bottom before they return.

Granddad's alarm clock goes off at six o' clock in the morning and they get up at the crack of dawn to give themselves plenty of time to do a thorough job. Barney is delighted to have a walk so early in the morning, but is not so happy when Rufus puts him on the lead, ties him to one of the mooring stakes and places a bowl of water within reach.

Starting with the outside they knuckle down to the task, washing the hull and scrubbing the decks, cleaning the windows and polishing the handrails. Granddad is using plenty of elbow grease and as the soft, cool glow of the rising sun gradually gives way to the full warmth of a bright, cloud free morning, he strips down to his vest.

Barney resigns himself to being tethered and falls asleep with his head resting on his paws.

When satisfied that the "Lady Jane" is looking shipshape, they move inside to pack their clothes into their suitcases and bags and put the few remaining groceries in a cardboard box. All Barney's bits and pieces are stuffed into a separate shopping bag. They sweep out the cabins and then mop the floors. All wrappers, empty bottles and other rubbish are placed in a large plastic bag and sealed. They wash up the breakfast things and clean the tabletop and the work surfaces in the galley, then they turn their attention to the washbasin, shower and toilet. Next they strip the beds and neatly fold up the linen.

At eleven 'o clock, with everything squared away, they step back and check that everything is spick and span.

"Job well done," declares Granddad, slipping on his shirt. "She looks as good as when we picked her up."

Rufus nods in agreement. "I don't know about you Granddad, but I'm really thirsty after all that work?"

"Me too," says Granddad, and stooping, he opens the refrigerator and takes out a bottle of lemonade. "I left this one in here so that we'd have something cold and refreshing when we were done."

He fills two tumblers with the fizzy drink and they sit outside in the sunshine on the cushioned seat.

A brightly painted narrow boat passes on its way downstream and as is the custom on the river everyone waves. Rufus watches it wistfully as it sails out of sight. Granddad, understanding his mood, puts an arm around his shoulder and draws him close.

"All good things come to an end, Ruuf, but nobody can take the memories away. We've had a wonderful holiday and now it's time to go home."

Barney is released and taken for a short run along the bank, but before he is allowed back on board, Rufus washes his feet in a bowl of water and dries them with a towel. After all their hard work they do not want him to make a mess.

"You can have the honour of sailing her on the last stretch," announces Granddad, jumping off to release the mooring lines.

As Rufus noses the "Lady Jane" into the entrance to the marina, Barney lets out a yelp as he spots Mum and Dad waiting on the jetty. At the same moment Mum and Dad's faces break into broad smiles and they wave.

Dad is absolutely amazed at how expertly Rufus guides the big cruiser smoothly between the other boats that are tightly packed along the quayside, and then, seemingly without effort or help from Granddad, brings her neatly to rest against the pontoon.

Granddad throws the mooring lines to Dad, who ties them off, then turns to Rufus and claps him on the back. "Couldn't have done it better myself shipmate."

Rufus switches off the engine and jumps onto the landing stage into Mum's open arms. She gives him a big hug and a kiss and then holds him at arms length. "My goodness! Look how brown you are, and I swear you've grown another inch. Have you had a lovely time? You've obviously had plenty of sunshine. Did you experience any of those terrible rainstorms?"

Dad shakes his head in amusement, "Give him a chance to get off the boat Mary," he laughs.

Mum crosses to Granddad and gives him a big hug and a kiss. "Thanks for looking after him Dad, and bringing him back safe and sound. You both look so fit and well, boating obviously suits the pair of you."

"They've had a right old time of it and no mistake!"

They all turn at the sound of Harry's voice.

"They've got sailing in their blood that's for sure, they just need to clue up a bit on navigating. Right Midge? "

He winks at Granddad.

Granddad feels uneasy, not knowing how much Harry has told Mum and Dad about their running aground on the riverbank, but there is no reaction from Mum, and Dad bends down to make a fuss of Barney.

Harry stops in his tracks. "My word!" he exclaims, staring at the "Lady Jane". "What have you done?"

Rufus darts a glance at Granddad.

"Well now, isn't that a pleasant surprise," Harry continues, standing in front of his prize boat. "I don't think I've ever seen her look so spotless."

"We've cleaned her inside and out," says Rufus eagerly. "We thought it would save you lots of time today."

"Well bless the pair of you."

After a quick look around inside he emerges and declares, "This calls for a cup of tea. I'll get Mavis to put the kettle on. When you've packed all your stuff in the car, come on up to the office. By the way young man," he turns to Rufus, "Mavis has got a big surprise for you!"

"Oh, what?"

"Just you wait and see," he says, winking and tapping the side of his nose.

Rufus is intrigued and curious to discover what Mavis' surprise might be and it does not take long before they have the car packed.

As he walks into the office it is Rufus' turn to be absolutely amazed. There, standing in the middle of Mavis' desk, is his red and yellow, model fishing boat. Rufus is overcome with joy and cannot believe it, but there it sits waiting for him.

Rufus gives Granddad Barney's lead.

Mavis carefully picks up the boat and hands it over. "You've got Margery Travers at the Post Office in Upper Filton to thank for this," she explains, in answer to Rufus' enquiring look.

"Somebody was fishing and found it caught in the reeds in Willow Brook and brought it into the Post Office. Margery recognised it straight away and realizing you would be returning to the marina today, she drove over yesterday afternoon to deliver it. She said to tell you that she is so pleased that your boat has been found and knows how disappointed you must have been to lose it."

Rufus turns to Granddad and holds the model up to show him.

"You'll have to send that nice Margery a thank you letter," says Granddad. "She's taken a lot of trouble to get it back to you."

"That really is kind and considerate," says Mum. "We'll send her a bunch of flowers, as a special thank you."

"Tea's up," calls Harry, coming in with a tray of steaming cups.

They say goodbye to Harry and Mavis, but before getting in the car Rufus walks back down the jetty for one last look at the "Lady Jane". Memories of the holiday come flooding back and he runs his hand lovingly along the sleek side of the cruiser.

Once Rufus is settled in the rear seat with Granddad and Barney, Dad starts the engine and they drive out of the marina through the double gates under the Smartboats sign.

"By the way," enquires Mum, turning round in her seat. "Did you both enjoy my large pot of strawberry jam?"

Rufus and Granddad look at each other, then Granddad replies, "Yes Mary, it was wonderful, we spread it on everything."

Mum gives a little smile of satisfaction and turns back.

All is quiet, then Granddad suddenly snorts and Rufus starts giggling and before long they are falling about on the back seat in helpless laughter with tears rolling down their cheeks.

Mum and Dad look at one another and wonder what on earth is going on.

UPSTREAM

STEP 1

Sail into the lock under the guillotine.

STEP 2

Lower the guillotine.

STEP 3

Fill the lock pen by opening the paddles.

STEP 4

Open the swing gates and sail out of the lock.

DOWNSTREAM

STEP 1

Fill the lock pen and open the swing gates.

STEP 2

Sail into the lock and close the swing gates.

STEP 3

Inch open the guillotine to empty the lock pen

STEP 4

Raise the guillotine to full height and sail out of the lock.

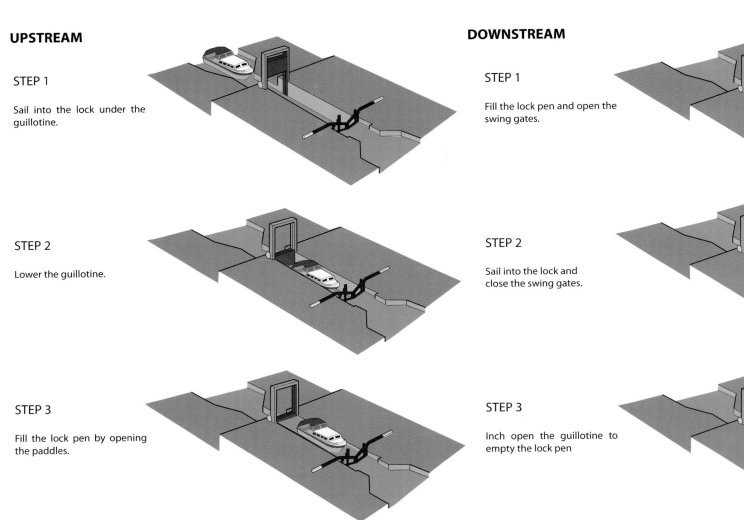
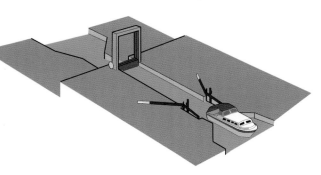
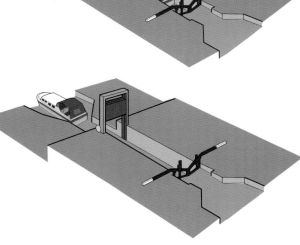

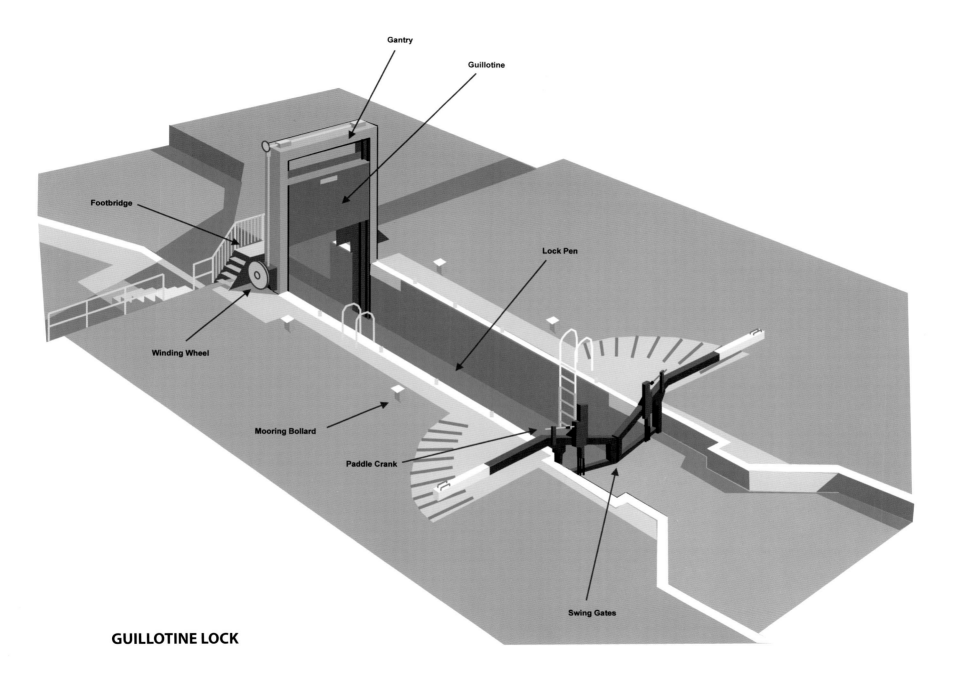

Gantry

Guillotine

Footbridge

Lock Pen

Winding Wheel

Mooring Bollard

Paddle Crank

Swing Gates

GUILLOTINE LOCK